Monster Tree House Club: Jayden's Homework Problem

By: Benjamin Hall

Illustrated by: Bri Sidari

Monster Tree House Club: Jayden's Homework Problem

First Edition Printed 2014

ISBN-13:
978-0692246399 (PT Publishing LLC)

ISBN-10:
0692246398

Bright yellow sun beams glossed through the window behind Jayden but he would not be going outside today to dance in the rays. Jayden was stuck in his desk chair looking down at a 12 math problems that seemed impossible to solve. He had only been there for 10 minutes but hadn't even begun the first problem and he felt like he would never be able to meet the children outside to play before the sun went down. Sounds of cheers and excited screams echoed in through the same window but still Jayden sat there growing more and more upset. Jayden liked school but he loved to play with his friends outside.

After what seemed like hours, Jayden's mother came home and found him frowning at his desk in his room.

"Jayden, haven't you finished your homework?" His mother asked as she kneeled down beside her very upset son.

"No...," Jayden muttered as he lifted one eyebrow towards her. His mother looked over the problems before him and wondered what could be the problem. "My homework is just too hard!"

"How was school today? Was the math work today really difficult?" his mother asked

"No!" Jayden exclaimed frustrated. His mother knew this meant Jayden just wanted to go outside but the rules were, homework first!

"Well try to get a few problems done while I fix you a

snack and I'll check on you then." Jayden's mother said as she walked off and this left Jayden more upset than before. He hoped his mom would take pity on him and let him play while there was still daylight left. Deciding that there was no hope of having fun if he didn't do the work, Jayden finally got his head into his math problems and completed his homework before his mom came back in with his sandwich and milk.

"Finished already?" His mother grinned as she sat down his plate on his desk but Jayden was already pulling on his socks and shoes. He grabbed his sandwich and guzzled down his milk before sprinting out the door. Had his mother blinked she would have missed him dashing across the lawn and into the backwoods where a game of hide and go seek was already in progress.

Jayden got to the woods and searched high and low for the other kids that he heard before he got to the thicket but found no one. He decided to climb a tree so he could scout out who was around. As he got about five feet in the air, he heard crunching of leaves and looked to find his friend Daniel beneath him. Daniel waved up to his brave bold friend Jayden and Jayden smiled down to Daniel as he climbed down.

“Hey where is everyone?” Jayden asked excitedly but Daniel shrugged. Daniel as pretty shy and usually didn’t participate in the games everyone did.

"I was just exploring the woods a bit but I think everyone ran to the street to play basketball." Daniel said as he pointed back towards the road. Jayden really wanted to play with the group but he didn't want to leave Daniel alone. He was new in town and didn't have too many friends but Jayden befriended him in school a few weeks ago. Grinning, he started walking ahead of Daniel and Daniel followed behind him, happy to have the company.

The pair chatted about different cartoons they loved and books Daniel had read about wizards and trolls. Jayden wasn't big into reading but he loved hearing about the adventures that Daniel loved to read about. They were so interested in talking that they didn't see the bushes about them moving them; something was following the boys! Out of nowhere popped a green creature with big claws and pointed teeth. It smiled at the boys but they thought it was an evil grin. The boys were very scared but frozen in their fear. They wanted to run so bad but their feet wouldn't let them. Jayden looked to Daniel and Daniel stood there closing his eyes and hoping that the creature would just go away.

The creature did not just go away though, he flapped his big ears as he got closer to investigate the boys. Jayden stood his ground bravely and in his loudest voice tried to roar. All that came out was a mere squeak though. The monster fell back on his butt and LAUGHED a very funny laugh. He held his furry green stomach and tears formed in its eyes from how hard he was giggling. He sat up after a few minutes to find two very confused little boys. Once they were scared now they didn't know what to think of the creature before them

"HI there!" The creature waved. The boys nervously waved back and looked at each other for reassurance.

"Hello." Jayden stammered, now deflated by the monster that had laughed at him.

"What are you guys doing?" The creature inquired.

"We were just exploring the woods. We didn't mean to upset you and we just want to go home." Jayden stated, trying to look serious. Poor Daniel was still shaking and very frightened. He would do anything to just run if he could muster the courage of his legs to do so.

“I’m not upset at all!” The monster smiled brightly. His teeth were no longer menacing but now his smile seemed welcoming.

“Then can we go?” Daniel cried weakly.

“I guess if you want, but I was loving the story about the wizards!” the monster chimed. This confused Daniel, he thought the monster wanted to eat them but instead he seemed intrigued by them. Daniel then realized the monster wasn’t following them to hurt them but to hear the story that Daniel was telling. Daniel reached around to his pack and pulled out his book to show the monster. He took a few small steps forward and sat down where the monster could see the pages of the book and began to read out loud. Jayden came in to close the circle and the three became completely enthralled in the story as Daniel got into the story telling. He used different voices for each character and would raise his voice in the exciting parts. Daniel had fun showing his new friend his favorite book.

Night came quicker than both boy thought it would though and the boys had to bid their new furry friend farewell for the evening. School the next day seemed to drag on for both boys as they wanted to be back in those woods to see if they could find the monster again. As they both got off the school bus, Jayden realized… he once again had to do homework. He was even more frustrated, he had no desire to think over problems when he wanted to go find this new curious creature he met the previous day

He sat down and frowned at the homework before him and felt like crying as he couldn't get himself into the mindset to do it. Soon an hour had pasted and he heard a knock on his front door. It was Daniel looking very hurried and flustered.

"Hi Daniel." Jayden sighed while opening the door, he knew Daniel would want to go outside.

“Ready to go to the woods?” Daniel whispered, he didn’t want Jayden’s mom to hear where they were going. Jayden thought about it for a second and decided to hide his homework in his backpack and just say it was done. He nodded at Daniel and disappeared into his room quickly to put his shoes on. He knew his mother and teacher would be very upset but he just knew he couldn’t miss the opportunity to see this new mysterious monster. The boys practically bounced off the ground as they went running breathlessly into the woods. Rushing to the tree they last saw the monster at they began to call out softly, scared other kids might hear them. The same snaps and cracks began to sound in their ears and the big furry green monster appeared but this time the boys were not as scared. Daniel pulled out his book and everyone sat down to read until the monster looked upon Jayden. He instantly frowned and his two big furry paws clapped together and his claws began to clank as they ran together. Both boys looked at the monster with a bit of fear and confusion as they didn't know why he would be so upset out of nowhere.

"Jayden, something is wrong." The monster said. Jayden couldn't figure out why the monster would ask such a question.

"Nothing is wrong." Jayden replied.

"Jayden what did you not do today?" the monster responded growing more concerned. Jayden paused, how did the monster know all this?

"My homework..." Jayden shrugged. The monster sat back on his rear end and twiddled his fingers more.

"Do you not realize how important homework is?" The monster inquired.

"Well I wanted to come out here to see you." Jayden offered in hopes that flattering the monster may make him forget about the homework and continue with the story. The monster stood straight up though and motioned for the boys to follow him. The boys were even more confused though but they started walking down the path further into the woods.

Stopping in a clearing, the boys looked about found nothing special about the place the monster had led them. The monster lifted his mighty paws up into the air and began to speak in a language that neither boy had ever heard but before their eyes they saw wood and bramble began to lift into the air and form a house in the trees. Little wooden planks attached to the tree forming steps and the monster began to crawl up the ladder. Jayden bravely followed behind and Daniel came close on his heels.

Inside the tree house were cute little chairs and a table. The boys were so high that they could see their homes from the windows. They loved this new place the monster had built. The monster was not celebrating with them though, he was busy again speaking the same strange language but now a puff of purple smoke filled the room and soon the boys could not see an inch in front of their faces.

As the smoke cleared, both boys didn't recognize each other or themselves. Daniel was now dressed head to toe as a wizard complete with hat and staff and Jayden was now a blue and green monster with three eyeballs.

They both jumped backwards and poor Daniel cried out in fear from the new monster before him.

"Daniel calm down, it's me your friend Jayden!" Jayden screamed over Daniel's loud shrieks. Daniel calmed down for a second but was still shaking. He couldn't believe his friend was this creature before him but before he could investigate further the green furry monster appeared before them. He started walking towards a village in the distance and both boys followed after him.

Jayden's feet thudded along as he kept stepping harder than he intended. Daniel wasn't struggling as much with his new look as it was really just a change of clothing for him. His problem was keeping up with the two monsters who took large steps but soon they were all at the village.

This was no normal village though, everything in it was a monster but none of them seemed to mind Jayden or Daniel. The monster walked around to each hut and field and the boys kept pace right along. They watched monsters working with wood as little monsters helped pick up the scraps and measure. They saw monsters milking cows and little monsters bringing new pails to fill with milk. They watched monsters cooking while little monsters stirred pots and brought the dishes to set the table. Everyone worked with such harmony and showed all the little monsters exactly how to do the job they were.

"This is my mom," the monster explained. "See here we all have to help each other and teach each other things to survive."

"This is so cool!" Jayden exclaimed, he loved the new place and watching these monsters as they went about their everyday lives. The children seemed more than happy to do whatever the adult monsters were doing; they loved learning.

"It is cool Jayden. If the adults didn't teach the children or if they children played all day and didn't take the time to learn then the village would fall apart. Someone has to teach them and they have to be willing to be taught." The monster pointed out. This struck Jayden hard as he realized that he hated doing his homework and it wasn't nearly as hard as the little monster hauling a large piece of lumber around. All he had to do was about 10 math problems a night and a bit of reading.

"But this stuff needs to be done..." Jayden tried to defend himself but knew he was wrong.

"So does your school work Jayden. What you learn in school will help you when you're grown up and you can use those skills to help your friends and family. No job is unimportant but without education you can't do any job!" The monster zipped back. It was in that moment that Jayden realized that even though it seemed unimportant, the work he was doing was helping him to help others later. The monster then started walking back in the direction they came and the boys very quickly followed suit. Daniel looked back and gave a quick wave to the monsters they were leaving behind. The little monsters all raised their paws to wave back but then the purple haze filled the air around them again and soon the boys found themselves back in the treehouse they started in. It was now night time and both boys had to hurry home.

The next day Jayden awoke early and finished the homework he had neglected. He hurried to school faster than his mother had ever seen and paid more attention in class than his teacher was ever used too. He just wanted to learn everything so that he could grow up one day to know as much as those adult monsters he had seen the previous day. When he got home to do his homework, though he was excited to see his new friend, he happily did his homework and found he finished it faster when he had a positive attitude about the work at hand. He finished long before Daniel came to knock on his door and was ready to race off into the woods to find their furry monster pal and go on a new adventure!

About the Author:

Benjamin Hall is the proud father of two with one more on the way and has a passion for reading. Serving in the US Army for 6 years, he has now turned his sights to helping encourage early childhood reading and education.

The Monster Tree House Club series was inspired by a combination of his childhood experiences, his children and nieces and nephews. Wanting to bring a new interactive way for children to engage with the world around them and understand new concepts the Monster Tree House was created!

Check out www.monstertreehouseclub.com to get personalized letters, personalized videos from the Tree House Monster and other books!

About the Illustrator:

Bri Sidari is an amazing artist and currently residing in Canada. Excelling in the 'chibi' style of illustration, she was the perfect choice of illustrator for the Monster Tree House Club series. Feel free to contact her at http://www.fiverr.com/beezies/draw-cute-chibi-version-of-you-or-any-character

About the Puppeteer:

Jack Thomas is an amazing voice actor and puppeteer! His voice really brings to live the Tree House Monsters that dwell within our realm. His love for inspiring children's creativity is truly boundless. Currently residing in the USA he loves to use his myriad of puppets to bring smiles and joy to all around him. He would love to do a personalized video just for you! Check him out at http://www.fiverr.com/derpsandwich/record-a-personal-video-using-a-furry-monster-puppet and mention that Monster Tree House Club sent you!

MONSTER TREE HOUSE CLUB: EDUCATION BY INSPIRING YOUNG MINDS

Thank you for your purchase! We would again like to invite you to join up at www.monstertreehouseclub.com with the coupon code at the beginning of the book. Join us on facebook at www.facebook.com/monstertreehouseclub and mention that you bought this book to get a scoop on our upcoming new book! That's right, more coupon codes for our upcoming book titles!

Monster Tree House Club: Kamia's Supporting Role (July 15th 2014)

Monster Tree House Club: Daniel the Shy Wizard (Coming SOON)

Monster Tree House Club: Dallas's New School (Coming SOON)

CPSIA information can be obtained
at www.ICGtesting.com
Printed in the USA
LVIC04n0036031015
456800LV00016B/68